Cat Days

D0029626

by Alexa Andrews
illustrated by John & Wendy

Penguin Young Readers
An Imprint of Penguin Group (USA) Inc.

Dear Parents and Educators,

Welcome to Penguin Young Readers! As parents and educators, you know that each child develops at his or her own pace—in terms of speech, critical thinking, and, of course, reading. Penguin Young Readers recognizes this fact. As a result, each Penguin Young Readers book is assigned a traditional easy-to-read level (1–4) as well as a Guided Reading Level (A–P). Both of these systems will help you choose the right book for your child. Please refer to the back of each book for specific leveling information. Penguin Young Readers features esteemed authors and illustrators, stories about favorite characters, fascinating nonfiction, and more!

Cat Days

LEVEL **1**

GUIDED
READING
LEVEL **B**

This book is perfect for an **Emergent Reader** who:
- can read in a left-to-right and top-to-bottom progression;
- can recognize some beginning and ending letter sounds;
- can use picture clues to help tell the story; and
- can understand the basic plot and sequence of simple stories.

Here are some **activities** you can do during and after reading this book:
- Word Families: Word families are groups of words that have common patterns. They have the same combinations of letters in them and sound alike. For example, *cat* and *hat* are a family of words. They have the *at* sound and letter combination in common. Come up with a list of other words in the "at" family.
- Story Extension: The stories in this book are about what a cat does during the day. What else does a cat do during the day? What could the author have added to the stories?

Remember, sharing the love of reading with a child is the best gift you can give!

—Bonnie Bader, EdM
  Penguin Young Readers program

*Penguin Young Readers are leveled by independent reviewers applying the standards developed by Irene Fountas and Gay Su Pinnell in *Matching Books to Readers: Using Leveled Books in Guided Reading*, Heinemann, 1999.

For Atticus and Boo, and your kitty, too!
—J & W

Penguin Young Readers
Published by the Penguin Group
Penguin Group (USA) Inc., 375 Hudson Street, New York, New York 10014, USA
Penguin Group (Canada), 90 Eglinton Avenue East, Suite 700, Toronto, Ontario M4P 2Y3, Canada
(a division of Pearson Penguin Canada Inc.)
Penguin Books Ltd., 80 Strand, London WC2R 0RL, England
Penguin Group Ireland, 25 St. Stephen's Green, Dublin 2, Ireland (a division of Penguin Books Ltd.)
Penguin Group (Australia), 250 Camberwell Road, Camberwell, Victoria 3124, Australia
(a division of Pearson Australia Group Pty. Ltd.)
Penguin Books India Pvt. Ltd., 11 Community Centre, Panchsheel Park, New Delhi—110 017, India
Penguin Group (NZ), 67 Apollo Drive, Rosedale, Auckland 0632, New Zealand
(a division of Pearson New Zealand Ltd.)
Penguin Books (South Africa) (Pty.) Ltd., 24 Sturdee Avenue, Rosebank,
Johannesburg 2196, South Africa

Penguin Books Ltd., Registered Offices: 80 Strand, London WC2R 0RL, England

Text copyright © 2012 by Penguin Group (USA) Inc. Illustrations copyright © 2012 by John & Wendy.
All rights reserved. Published by Penguin Young Readers, an imprint of Penguin Group (USA) Inc.,
345 Hudson Street, New York, New York 10014. Manufactured in China.

Library of Congress Cataloging-in-Publication Data is available.

ISBN 978-0-448-46305-6   10

Cat Sits

Cat sits on the hat.

Do not sit on the hat, Cat.

Cat sits on the box.

Do not sit on the box, Cat.

Cat sits on the car.

Do not sit on the car, Cat.

Cat sits on the mat.

Sit on the mat, Cat.

Cat Plays

Cat plays with the bug.

The bug flies away.

Cat plays with the ball.

The ball rolls away.

Cat plays with the frog.

The frog hops away.

Cat plays with the dog.

The dog stays to play.

Cat Days

Cat can play.

Cat can run.

Run, Cat, run.

Cat can sit.

Cat can nap.

Nap, Cat, nap.